S0-BUB-842

REGINALD
THE STINKY
DOG

WRITTEN BY
KATHERINE RAWSON

ILLUSTRATED BY
MAX STASIUK

PIONEER VALLEY EDUCATIONAL PRESS, INC.

CONTENTS

CHAPTER 1
REGINALD

Reginald wasn't always a stinky dog. In fact, most of the time he was like any other dog. He took naps in the sun. He chased sticks and chewed shoes. He wagged his tail and barked when he was excited, and he growled when strangers came to the door.

Like most other dogs, Reginald loved his family. He loved to lick their faces when they hugged him, and he loved to nap with them on the sofa. Most of all, he loved to play with Amy and Jack.

The afternoon was Reginald's favorite time of day. That's when Amy and Jack came home from school. As soon as they opened the door, Reginald would wag his tail wildly. He would lick their faces as they hugged him and gave him treats.

Then he would run outside to play soccer with Amy and Jack and their friends. All the children loved playing soccer with Reginald. He loved to chase the ball and bark at it. He always had a wonderful time.

Reginald was a friendly dog,
and everyone loved to be with him.
They loved it most of the time,
but not all the time.

Sometimes Reginald was
a stinky dog. And when Reginald
got stinky, he got very, VERY stinky.

CHAPTER 2
MUD

One Saturday, Reginald decided to go for a walk by the river. There was always something interesting to do there. There were squirrels to chase, fish to catch, and sticks to find. Best of all, there was lots of stinky mud to roll around in.

Reginald loved to find sticks and bury them. That morning, he found a large stick on the ground. He dragged it over to the river bank where the mud was very soft. Then he began to dig. He dug and dug and dug.

Stinky mud covered his paws
and splashed all over his chest.
But Reginald didn't care. He kept
on digging. When the hole was deep
and wide, he dropped the stick in,
and covered it with lots of stinky
mud. He rolled in the mud some
more, and then scurried off to find
another stick.

By the end of the morning,
Reginald was covered with stinky
mud from his snout to his tail.

After all that digging
and burying, Reginald felt tired
and hungry. He thought about
his home. He thought about
his food dish, and his soft bed
in the corner of the kitchen.
He thought, "It's time
to go home!" He left the river
and headed toward his house.

At the street corner, Reginald
saw several people waiting
at the traffic light. He stopped
to wait, too.

"Ewwwww!" the people cried.
"What's that terrible stink?" They
all pinched their noses. When the
light changed, they hurried across
the road. Reginald hurried, too.
He wanted to get home to his
food dish.

"What a horrible stink!"
the people cried as they rushed
down the street.

Reginald rushed, too. He was still
thinking about his food dish.

"That awful stink is following us!"
the people cried, and they ran
even faster.

"I wonder if my food dish
is full," thought Reginald.
And he ran faster, too.

At the next corner, the people
rushed across the street as fast
as they could go. Reginald
turned right, and headed
up the block to his house.

CHAPTER 3
LOCKED OUT

Reginald ran toward his house, thinking about his food dish. He imagined it full of delicious food. He licked his chops and ran even faster.

Reginald ran to the kitchen door and looked through the screen. He saw his food dish on the floor. He scratched the door and barked loudly. "Hurry! Hurry!" his bark seemed to say.

Amy and Jack came to the door.
"Ewwwww! What's that awful stink?"
asked Jack.

"It's Reginald," said Amy.
"He's all muddy and stinky!"

"Don't let that stinky dog
in the house," their mother
yelled from the next room.

"You're stinky, Reginald," said
Jack. "Stay outside!" he yelled
as he slammed the door shut.

Reginald sat on the step. He
was very hungry, but his food dish
was inside and the door was shut.
 What could he do?

Reginald had nowhere to go,
so he started walking down
the street. He passed three children
playing in the yard next door.

"Ewwwww! What a terrible stink!"
they cried. They ran inside
and slammed the door.

Reginald just kept on going.
He saw a woman walking
down the street toward him.
"Dreadful, dreadful stink!" she cried
as Reginald came near her.
She pinched her nose and hurried
past him as quickly as she could.

21

Bang! Bang! Bang! All up and down the street, people slammed their doors and closed their windows. People scurried across the street as fast as they could go. No one wanted to be near such a terribly stinky dog!

Reginald kept on walking. He noticed he had the street all to himself, until suddenly, he heard a growl. He looked around, but he didn't see another dog anywhere.

Then he heard the growl again.
And again. It was very close.
The sound was so close it seemed
to be inside Reginald.

It was! The growl was coming
from Reginald's own stomach!
He was so hungry his stomach
was growling.

Just then, Reginald smelled
something delicious in the air.
He sniffed and sniffed. The delicious
smell reminded him of meat
and gravy. Yum!
His stomach growled loudly.

CHAPTER 4
LUNCH!

Reginald trotted down the block, following the delicious smell.
It took him around the corner, across the street, and down the next block, until it brought him to a glass door. Above the door was a sign that read:

Downtown Diner.

Reginald couldn't read the sign, but his nose knew what was on the other side of the door — meat and gravy!

Reginald sat down in front of the door and whined softly. How could he get to the meat and gravy?

Just then, the door opened. A tall man came out and glanced at Reginald. Then he covered his nose with his handkerchief and hurried away. Reginald didn't pay any attention to the man. He ran quickly through the open door, following the delicious smell of meat and gravy.

Inside, the diner was filled
with people, sitting on stools
by a tall counter.
There was a plate filled
with food in front of every person.

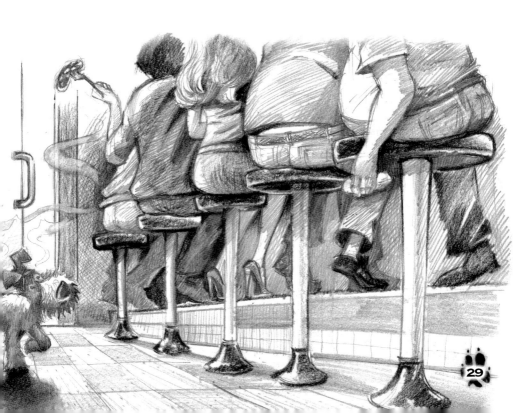

When Reginald walked through
the diner, the delicious smell
of meat and gravy filled his nose.
But the people on the stools
smelled something else.

"What's that awful stink?" someone
cried. "Ewwwww! How nasty!"
"Dis-gust-ing!" They all covered
their noses with their napkins
and rushed out the door.

Now all the stools were empty.
Reginald jumped up onto
a stool and looked at all
the delicious food on the counter.

He saw plates of meatloaf and gravy, hot turkey sandwiches, hamburgers, ham slices, and roast beef. Yum! And there were no people to eat all this delicious food. Reginald had it all to himself.

"It's not so bad being a stinky dog," he thought. He jumped up on the counter and began to eat.

Reginald gobbled up the food
and licked every plate clean.
When he got to the last plate,
he was certainly not hungry anymore!
He surveyed the row
of empty plates.

"A job well done," he thought
with satisfaction.

Then the door squeaked open,
and a new customer walked in
to the diner. She saw the counter
covered with empty plates
and muddy paw prints. She saw
Reginald sitting on the last stool
with a satisfied look on his face.
She noticed the awful stink.

"Oh! Oh!" she cried. She pinched her nose and rushed out the door. Reginald bounded out the door behind her. It was time for him to go home.

CHAPTER 5
SPRINKLER

Reginald trotted happily
down the street. He felt good
after his delicious meal.
The sun was shining, and the air
was warm. It was a beautiful day.

Soon he came to a house
with a pretty green lawn. He saw
a boy and a girl playing
in the yard. They were running
all around, jumping through jets
of water as water squirted
out of a lawn sprinkler.

"That looks like fun!"
thought Reginald. With a joyful
bark, he raced into the yard
and ran through the water
with the children.

The children turned to look
at Reginald. "Ewwwww!
What a stinky dog!" they cried.
They ran into the house
and slammed the door.

But Reginald didn't care.
He ran through the water
and barked with happiness.
The water felt cool on his nose.
It felt wonderful on his paws
and on his back.

The water began to wash the mud off Reginald's fur. Reginald ran and barked, and ran and barked some more. The more he played in the water, the more the mud washed off all the parts of his body. Soon there was not one spot of stinky mud left on him.

Reginald shook his fur, spraying
drops of clean water all over
the green lawn. Then he continued
walking down the street. Soon,
the sun dried his damp coat.
His fur got fluffy in the sunshine,
and he smelled sweet and clean.

Reginald saw a woman coming
down the street toward him. "What
a pretty dog!" she exclaimed,
and she stopped to scratch
Reginald's ears. He licked her hand.
"Oh, he kissed me!" the woman said,
and she scratched Reginald's ears
some more.

A boy came running out of the house on the corner. "It's Reginald!" he cried. "Want to play ball with me, Reginald?" The boy kicked a soccer ball to Reginald. Reginald chased the ball and tried to grab it with his teeth.

Just then a girl came down the street. "Isn't that dog Reginald?" she asked the boy.

"Yes. He belongs to Amy and Jack," the boy replied.

"Amy and Jack!" Reginald thought. They must be worried about him. They didn't know where he was! He dropped the ball and scampered down the street toward home.

"Reginald! Come back and play with us!" the boy and girl called. But Reginald kept running.

CHAPTER 6
HOME AGAIN

Reginald raced home. When
he reached the kitchen door,
he was panting hard.
He scratched the screen
and barked.

"It's Reginald!" cried Amy,
as she opened the door.

"Reginald's home!" Jack shouted
happily.

"We thought you were lost!"
said Amy. She hugged Reginald
and buried her face in his fur.

"I told you not to let that stinky dog in the house," their mother called from the other room.

"He's not stinky," said Jack.

"He smells wonderful," said Amy.

"He's been gone all day,"
said Jack. "He must be starving."
Jack piled dog food
into Reginald's dish
and set it down in front of him.

Reginald sniffed his dish, but his
stomach was full of meatloaf
and gravy, hot turkey sandwiches,
hamburgers, and delicious roast beef.
There wasn't room for anything else.
He sat by his dish and just looked
at Amy and Jack,
swishing his tail slowly.

44

"What's the matter, Reginald?"
asked Amy. "Don't you like
your chow?"

"He's not hungry," said Jack.
"I bet he wants to play."
Jack picked up his soccer ball.
"Come on, Reginald. Let's go
play soccer!"

But Reginald didn't want to play.
It had been a long day. He walked
slowly over to his soft bed
in the corner, turned around twice,
and plopped down comfortably.

"He's tired!" said Amy.

Amy and Jack sat by Reginald
and scratched his ears
until he fell asleep. And while
he slept, Reginald dreamed
happy dreams of meatloaf and gravy,
lawn sprinklers, soccer balls,
and sticks buried in soft, stinky mud.